The Twilight Fairies

for Ruby Barron,
with lots of love

Special thanks
to Sue Mongredien

ORCHARD BOOKS
338 Euston Road, London NW1 3BH
*Orchard Books Australia*
Level 17/207 Kent Street, Sydney, NSW 2000
A Paperback Original

First published in 2010 by Orchard Books

© 2010 Rainbow Magic Limited.
A HIT Entertainment company. Rainbow Magic
is a trademark of Rainbow Magic Limited.
Reg. U.S. Pat. & Tm. Off. And other countries.

HiT entertainment

Illustrations © Orchard Books 2010

A CIP catalogue record for this book is available
from the British Library.

ISBN 978 1 40830 909 4

1 3 5 7 9 10 8 6 4 2

Printed in China by Imago

The paper and board used in this paperback are natural recyclable
products made from wood grown in sustainable forests. The
manufacturing processes conform to the environmental regulations
of the country of origin.

Orchard Books is a division of Hachette Children's Books,
an Hachette UK company

www.hachette.co.uk

# Morgan
## the Midnight Fairy

by Daisy Meadows

ORCHARD BOOKS

www.rainbowmagic.co.uk

The Fairyland Palace

Observatory

Game Are

Fairy Homes

Ferry

CAMP STAR GAZE

Mirror Lake

The Twinkling Tree

Starry Glade

Jack Frost's Ice Castle

BBQ

Picnic Area

Stream

Tree top Walk

Bridge

Zip Slides

FOREST FUN ADVENTURE PLAYGROUND

Tree House

Wildlife Hide

Whispering Wood

The Twilight Fairies' magical powers
Bring harmony to the night-time hours.
But now their magic belongs to me,
And I'll cause chaos, you shall see!

Sunset, moonlight and starlight too,
There'll be no more sweet dreams for you,
From evening dusk to morning light
I am the master of the night!

# Contents

# The Midnight Hour

"I'm not tired at all, are you?" Kirsty Tate asked her best friend Rachel Walker. It was late at night and the two girls were in the Whispering Wood, collecting firewood. They were staying with their families at a holiday centre called Camp Stargaze, and tonight the whole camp were having a midnight feast together.

"Not a bit," Rachel replied, tugging at a branch from the undergrowth. "I'm way too excited to even think about being tired!" She grinned at Kirsty.

"What a brilliant holiday this is turning out to be. A whole week together, lots of adventures, a midnight feast and…" She lowered her voice, glancing around cautiously. "And plenty of fairy magic, too!"

Kirsty smiled. It was true – she and Rachel had been having a wonderful time so far this week.

On their very first evening in camp,

they'd met Ava the Sunset Fairy, who was one of seven Twilight Fairies. The Twilight Fairies looked after the world between dusk and dawn, making sure that everything was as it should be with the help of their special bags of magical dust. But a few nights ago, naughty Jack Frost had stolen these bags while the seven fairies were having a party together.

Kirsty and Rachel were friends with the fairies and had had lots of exciting adventures with them before, so when the Twilight Fairies asked if they would help search for the stolen fairy dust, Kirsty and Rachel were happy to say yes.

So far they had found three bags of
magic dust belonging to Ava the Sunset
Fairy, Lexi the Firefly Fairy and Zara
the Starlight Fairy, but there were still
four left to find.

It was a chilly night and Kirsty and

Rachel were
pleased to
see that the
moon and
stars were
shining
brightly.

"Zara's starlight
magic is working perfectly again," Kirsty
said, gazing up at the twinkling stars.
She gathered some more sticks,
humming cheerfully to herself.

It was going to be such fun tonight!

A big fire was being lit, and then there would be lots of fireworks on the stroke of midnight, followed by a feast for everyone.

As the girls made their way through the dark wood, they heard a voice calling: "Kirsty, Rachel, is that you? We've found loads of firewood down here!"

"Follow our torchlights!" shouted a second voice, and then the girls saw bright white beams of light flashing through the trees in the distance.

"Sounds like Lucas and Matt," Rachel said. "Come on, let's find them."

"We're on our way!" Kirsty called. She and Rachel had become good friends with Lucas and Matt while they'd been at the camp, and had had a lot of fun together so far.

Before long, Rachel and Kirsty saw a grove ahead, with Lucas and Matt standing in the middle, still waving their torchlights around.

"Be careful," Matt warned. "The path gets a bit slippery, so—"

Just as he said the words, Rachel felt her foot skid on some pine needles that lay on the track. She clutched at Kirsty to get her balance but couldn't help slipping. "Whoa!" she yelled, losing her footing completely and bumping down on her bottom. She accidentally pulled Kirsty over too, and they both dropped their firewood as they slipped and slid down into the grove with a bump-bump-BUMP!

Luckily they landed on soft cushions of moss, and were unhurt. Lucas and Matt helped them up, then they all set about collecting the dropped firewood together.

"It's pretty down here, isn't it?" Kirsty said, shining her torch about. The glade was circular, with tall pine trees around it, and, as she swung the torch's beam along the ground, she saw that there were hundreds of tiny, white, star-shaped flowers dotting the velvety green moss.

"It's called Starry Glade," Matt told them. "Because of those star-shaped flowers, I guess. Or maybe because when you look up at night, all you can see is the stars."

"And fireworks, too, tonight," Lucas reminded him. "Come on, let's take this firewood back. It can't be too much longer until midnight!"

# Sparks Fly!

Rachel, Kirsty, Lucas and Matt headed back to the large clearing where the other campers had gathered. The adults were preparing the campfire for the midnight feast and had built a large pile of sticks, surrounded by a ring of stones.

"Make sure you children stay outside this stone ring," Peter, one of the camp leaders, told them. "Once we get the fire blazing, it's going to be very hot, and there may be flying sparks." He patted his pockets. "Talking of lighting the fire… I'd better get on with it. Where did I put those matches?"

Kirsty and Rachel set their firewood on a pile nearby while Peter went on searching for the matches. "I'm sure I packed them," he muttered, rifling through his pack. "Where are they?"

Kirsty's dad grabbed a couple of dry sticks. "I wasn't in the cub scouts for nothing," he said, rubbing them together. "I'll have a spark in a minute, and we can get that fire going."

Unfortunately, no spark appeared despite Mr Tate's best efforts, and Peter still couldn't find his matches. A few minutes later, Rachel's parents came into the clearing carrying boxes of food for the feast. "Oh!" said Mrs Walker in surprise. "I thought the fire would be lit by now. We'll have to hurry if we're going to cook these sausages."

Rachel explained the problem, and her mum smiled. "Don't worry," she said, "I've got some matches in my emergency kit. Let me see… Here!"

Everyone broke into applause as Mrs Walker triumphantly held up the matchbox, and Peter wasted no time in striking a match and getting the fire alight.

Kirsty and Rachel sat on a nearby log to watch. Despite the huge mountain of firewood that had been collected, the fire stayed disappointingly small.

The flames crept along the twigs but failed to catch on any of the larger branches. Smoke billowed into the air, making people cough and choke.

"Let's get cooking," Mr Walker said, loading up a pan with sausages and onions and balancing it on the fire. He winked at Rachel and Kirsty. "You can't beat the smell of sausages sizzling on a campfire, that's what I say!" But unfortunately, even after quite a while, the sausages were not sizzling and still looked pink and raw. "They don't seem to be cooking at all," Mr Walker frowned. "I don't think the fire is hot enough."

"Shall we try toasting the marshmallows instead?" Kirsty suggested, feeling hungry. She and Rachel had found some special long thin sticks that looked especially good for marshmallow-toasting.

"Great idea," Mrs Tate said, tearing open the marshmallow bags and passing them around. Everyone threaded marshmallows onto their sticks, before carefully holding them in the campfire.

"I love the way the outsides get crunchy, while the insides are lovely and gooey," Rachel said, watching her marshmallow as the flames flickered around it. "But you mustn't leave it in too long, remember. Burned marshmallows are not so tasty!"

"No," Kirsty agreed. "The moment it turns brown, you need to whip it out – and gobble it up!"

The girls waited and waited for their marshmallows to toast but they stayed pink and white for a surprisingly long time. "They must be ready by now," Rachel said, taking hers out of the fire and testing it cautiously against her lips. "Oh," she said in surprise. "It's still cold!"

Kirsty tried hers – and so did the other campers. Their marshmallows were cold, too! What was going on? Why wasn't the fire cooking anything?

"The Midnight Feast is going to be a midnight flop at this rate," Mr Tate said in dismay. People nearby were muttering grumpily about feeling tired and wanting to go to bed. "Maybe this wasn't such a good idea after all."

Just then the fire crackled loudly as a log split right down the middle, and glowing sparks flew up into the dark sky. Everybody backed off, including Rachel and Kirsty, not wanting to be burned by a hot spark.

As they stepped away from the fire, the girls saw that one of the sparks seemed to be headed straight for them.

They dodged to the side, and the spark whizzed off into the darkness and vanished. As it flew past them, Kirsty noticed that the 'spark' had shimmering silver wings. "That's no spark," she hissed to Rachel. "It's Morgan the Midnight Fairy!"

# A Spooky Story

Kirsty and Rachel had met all seven of
the Twilight Fairies on the first day of
their adventure, and felt very excited as
they slipped away from the campfire,
in the direction Morgan had flown.
"There she is, on that tree stump!"
Rachel whispered, hurrying towards
the little fairy.

Morgan waved and fluttered up into
the air as the girls
approached.
    She had blonde
hair in a sweet,
elfin crop, with
a midnight-blue
hairband, and wore
a pretty dark blue
dress of floaty chiffon
that swung out as she flew,
with matching sparkly, peep-toe shoes.
    Rachel quickly pulled open her coat
pocket so that Morgan could fly inside
and wouldn't be seen by anybody else.
She and Kirsty still had their backs to the
fire so that they could talk to Morgan in
secret. "Hello," she whispered. "Nice to
see you again!"

"You too," Morgan replied. "But I'm sorry the midnight feast isn't going well. As the Midnight Fairy, I can usually make midnight feasts and parties really wonderful and exciting, with the help of my magic night dust. Since Jack Frost stole it, though, midnight parties have been going wrong all over the world, and in Fairyland too."

Kirsty nodded. "Our fire hasn't lit properly, and isn't cooking the food. People are getting really fed up, and are even talking about going to bed."

"And that would be such a shame, because we've got fireworks planned for midnight," Rachel added.

Morgan looked anxious. "Then I really must find my night dust before then," she said. "If I don't, I know already the fireworks will be a total let-down."

Peter clapped his hands loudly just

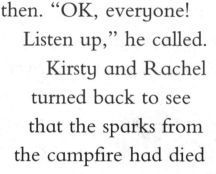

then. "OK, everyone! Listen up," he called. Kirsty and Rachel turned back to see that the sparks from the campfire had died away, and that everyone was sitting on logs around the fire once more. They sat down quickly, too.

"To get everyone in a spooky mood for midnight, we'll go around the circle, taking it in turns to tell part of a ghost story," Peter went on. "I'll start things off." He cleared his throat.

"Once upon a time, it was a dark, stormy night, and two children were lost in the woods…"

Rachel shivered delightedly. She loved ghost stories! But as the story passed around the circle, it began to get rather silly.

"… And they met a giant…sheep," a boy called Jake giggled. "And the sheep gave a big sneeze, and all its wool fell off on the children's heads!"

Jake's big sister, Laura, pulled a face. "Jake! Don't mess about," she told him. "Do it properly."

Jake shrugged. "That's all I can think of," he replied. "I'm too tired to make up a story anyway."

"We're all tired and cold but there's no need to—" Laura began arguing.

"OK, OK," Peter interrupted quickly. "Let's not bicker. A giant sheep is fine. Kirsty, do you want to add a bit of the story? What happens next? And make it scary!"

"Um…" Kirsty said. "The children pulled the sheep's wool off their heads and went further into the forest," she said, thinking fast. "Then something really scary happened."

"What?" Lucas interrupted.

"The children saw…" Kirsty's mind went blank. She had no idea what could happen next! She tried to think of the most terrifying thing she'd ever seen in her life, and then before she could stop herself, she blurted out, "The children saw JACK FROST!"

Rachel gasped. "Kirsty!" she hissed warningly. She and Kirsty were meant to keep their fairy adventures secret as no humans were meant to know about Fairyland or its magical inhabitants. And that included Jack Frost!

Kirsty clapped a hand to her mouth.

"Sorry," she whispered. "It just came out."

Thankfully in the next moment, Matt gave a cry. "There's a monster!" he yelled, pointing into the shadowy bushes with a shaking finger. "I saw a monster running along over there. It had a long nose and big feet, and it was g-g-g-green!"

Peter laughed, thinking Matt was joking and this was all part of the story. Some of the other grown-ups laughed as well. "There are no such things as monsters!" Matt's mum told him. "It's just your imagination."

But Kirsty and Rachel didn't laugh – they looked at each other in dismay. They were sure that the green thing Matt had described wasn't a monster, or "just his imagination". It had to be one of Jack Frost's sneaky goblins!

# Gobbling Goblins

"Shall we get some more firewood?" Rachel asked, getting to her feet. "I could do with stretching my legs."

"Me too," Kirsty said, standing up beside her. Like Rachel, she was keen to find out what the goblin was doing in the Whispering Wood. Goblins were slippery, untrustworthy creatures and the one that Matt had seen was sure to be up to no good!

"OK," Rachel's dad said. "Watch out for monsters, though," he joked.

Kirsty and Rachel set off in the direction where Matt said he'd seen the monster. Once they were safely hidden by the trees, Morgan fluttered out from Rachel's pocket. "That was a goblin your friend spotted," she told them.

"I saw him myself, and he seemed in a great hurry. I wonder what's going on?" She took out her wand. "Let's fly further into the wood and see if we can find him."

She waved her wand over the girls and
a stream of fairy magic swirled out of it,
glittering with tiny golden clock-shapes.
As the magic tumbled around Kirsty
and Rachel, they
felt themselves
shrinking
smaller
and
smaller,
until they
were the
same size
as Morgan.
They both had
their very own pair of sparkling fairy
wings on their backs, and with a few
quick flutters, they were up in the air,
as high as the tree-tops.

The wood was bathed in silver moonlight and looked wonderfully magical, Kirsty thought as she flew. An owl hooted softly somewhere nearby and the leaves rustled in the trees below.

After a short while, they heard footsteps and Rachel pointed downwards. "There he is!" she said, spotting the goblin who was skipping along happily. They hung back behind him and followed him through the trees. It wasn't long before they could smell yummy cooking smells, and hear cheerful singing.

The goblin led them all the way to a clearing where a whole gang of other goblins were sitting around a campfire, obviously about to have their own midnight feast. This was a much jollier feast than the one Rachel and Kirsty had just come from: the fire blazed merrily, and the goblins

who weren't singing were tucking in to hot dogs and jacket potatoes cooked by the heat of the flames.

"Delicious," one goblin said, cramming
the rest of his hot dog into his mouth
and chewing hard. Crumbs sprayed
everywhere and Rachel and Kirsty
pulled faces at each other. Yuck!

"And what I fancy next," the same
goblin said, taking a dark blue satin bag
and opening the drawstrings, "is some
bogmallows. Give me bogmallows!"

Morgan gasped. "That's my bag of
magic night dust!" she whispered to
Kirsty and Rachel.

They watched as the goblin plunged
his hand into the satin bag and took out
a pinch of sparkling dust. He sprinkled
the dust into the air…and then, with
a golden shimmering light, a large pile
of green marshmallows appeared next
to him.

Rachel and Kirsty had seen green marshmallows like this before when they'd helped Gabriella the Snow Kingdom Fairy on another adventure, and knew that they were goblin sweets called 'bogmallows'. The goblin whooped. "Woo-hooo! Bogmallows, everyone! Come and get them!"

He reached into the bag and sprinkled more fairy dust, making another large pile of bogmallows. The goblins crowded around with big sticks, shoving the bogmallows on three at a time before toasting them.

"Wow," Kirsty breathed. "That's a lot of bogmallows!"

"And a waste of magic dust," Morgan fumed. "We've got to get my bag back, before he uses up the lot!"

"Let me have a go with that dust," another goblin with a squeaky voice said, trying to snatch it. "I want to magic up more sausages."

"No!" the first goblin said, jerking the bag out of reach. "You've had plenty of sausages, don't be greedy."

"I'm thirsty," a third goblin put in. He tried to grab the bag, too. "Give that here and I'll magic us some more pop."

"No!" the first goblin said again. "It's mine and you're not getting it." And with that, he put the bag on the log and sat quickly on top of it, so that the bag was completely covered by his bottom.

Rachel's face fell. "How are we going to get the bag now?" she wondered anxiously. "Quick – we've got to think of a plan!"

# Boo!

"We need to get him off that log," Kirsty said, thinking aloud. "Maybe if he saw something exciting – or scary! – he would jump to his feet. Hmmm…"

"I've got it!" Rachel exclaimed. "We frighten him from his seat…by telling him a ghost story!"

"That's a great idea," Morgan said. "But wait…if we fly in like this, the goblins will know we're trying to get my bag back. We need disguises."

"Could you use your magic to make me look like a goblin?" Kirsty suggested. "Then I could sit down with them and tell them a spooky story."

"Yes," said Rachel. Her words tumbled out enthusiastically as she thought of something else. "And maybe if I'm disguised as a ghost, I could pop out when you get to the scariest bit, Kirsty – and I'll make all the goblins jump!"

The three friends grinned at each other.

"Perfect," Morgan said, and they flew down to land behind a thick bush so that she could work some fairy magic without being seen. She waved her wand, and once again, a stream of glittering sparkles swirled out from it, floating all around Kirsty and Rachel. Moments later, Kirsty felt herself growing taller, and her nose and ears became much bigger and pointier.

Rachel giggled. "You look just like a goblin!" she said.

Kirsty's eyes widened as she saw Rachel. "Is that really you?" she gasped. "You look so scary!"

Rachel had been turned into a ghostly figure – a shapeless, white, gleaming ghost, with dark mournful eyes and mouth. "Good," she said, at Kirsty's words. "Let's go and scare those goblins!"

"Try to do it quickly," Morgan advised. "These disguises use up a lot of magic and they won't last for very long. Good luck!"

Rachel hid behind a tree, while Kirsty joined the goblin group, trying to look as casual as possible. Really, her heart was pounding fast as she stood near the goblin who was sitting on the bag of magic dust. "Time for a ghost story!" she announced. "Is everyone listening?"

The goblins seemed pleased to be having a story, and they sat down obediently at once, all eyes on Kirsty.

Morgan ⚬⚬⚬⚬⚬⚬

"Once upon a time…" Kirsty began
in a low, spooky voice. She told them
a story about a haunted house where
ghostly Pogwurzels lurked (goblins were
very scared of Pogwurzels), and it wasn't
long before her audience were shivering
and clutching at each other for comfort.

"The goblin crept through the house,"
Kirsty went on, dropping her voice even
lower. "And then, all of a sudden…"

"BOO!" shouted Rachel, leaping out
from behind the tree.

"Aarrrrrghhh!" screamed the goblins,
all jumping up in fright. "Help!"

This was Morgan's cue to swoop in

and grab her bag of magic dust, but
just then, one of the goblins pointed at
Rachel and shouted, "Hey! That's not
a ghost – it's
a pesky girl!"

Kirsty gulped.
Oh no!
Rachel's magic
disguise was
wearing off –
and as she glanced
down at herself, she realised hers was
too! "Quick, Morgan!" she called out –
but she was too late. The goblin who'd
been sitting on the
bag whirled around and grabbed it
before Morgan could reach it, and rushed
out of the campfire ring, followed by the
rest of his gang.

Morgan promptly waved her wand
and turned Kirsty and Rachel back into
fairies. "After them!" she called. "Come
on!"

The three fairies soared after the racing
goblins, who were charging through the
dark wood at top speed. Rachel, Kirsty
and Morgan soon spotted the goblin with
the bag right at the front of the pack.
He glanced over his shoulder, and
a nervous look came over
his face as he saw the
three fairies flying
determinedly after
him. "Here – have
this!" he shouted,
tossing the bag of
magic dust to one
of his friends.

This goblin caught the bag, but just as Rachel, Kirsty and Morgan were making a beeline for him, he threw it on to another goblin, who caught it and kept on running.

So the chase went on through the woods with the goblins nimbly throwing the bag to one another, and the fairies becoming more and more frustrated as they swerved from goblin to goblin, trying to keep up. Dry sticks and leaves snapped beneath the goblins' big flat feet as they thudded along between the trees.

Rachel was beginning to feel despairing. How were they going to get Morgan's bag back with so many goblins? Then her gaze flicked to the stars that were twinkling in the night sky, and they reminded her of all the tiny white flowers she and Kirsty had seen in Starry Glade earlier that evening. It seemed ages since the two of them had gone skidding down the hill there.

"Wait!" she hissed to Kirsty and Morgan, as an idea popped into her head. "I've just thought of something! Remember how

58

we fell down that steep slope into Starry Glade earlier?" Kirsty nodded. "Well, if we could lead the goblins round that way, there's a chance they might slip down the hill, just like we did," Rachel went on. "And if they do..."

"We can fly in and grab my bag of night dust!" Morgan finished with a smile. "I know the glade you mean, and we're not far away. Come  on, let's see if your plan works."

The fairies caught up with the goblins as they raced along, and every time the path forked, Morgan would zip ahead and hover at the start of the fork they didn't want the goblins to go down.

"Give me my bag!" she'd call, with her
hands on her hips.

"No chance!" the goblins would retort,
veering off down the other path. Then
Kirsty, Rachel and Morgan would high-
five each other in secret. This was just
what they wanted!

Eventually, they steered the goblins
onto the path that ran down to Starry
Glade. Kirsty, Rachel and Morgan
whizzed over their heads. "I can see the
bag!" Kirsty cried loudly. "Let's get it!"

The goblin carrying the bag looked panicky at her words and glanced round for someone to throw it to.

But as he took his gaze from the path, he skidded on the slippery pine needles – letting go of Morgan's bag, and sending it flying into the air!

# Feast of Fun

Rachel and Kirsty immediately soared towards the bag, while Morgan used her magic to turn it into its usual Fairyland size. "Caught it!" cheered Kirsty, grabbing hold of the satiny material, and flying up high with it again.

Below them the goblins were slipping and sliding and falling over one another in a tangle of arms and legs, and Kirsty and Rachel beamed as Morgan flew over to join them. "Oh, well done!" Morgan exclaimed, taking the bag and hugging both Kirsty and Rachel in turn. "And just in time – it's nearly midnight!" She grinned. "Come on, let's leave these goblins here, and hurry back to your midnight feast. We might be able to turn it into a feast of fun after all!" She took out a pinch of her night dust and muttered some magic words that sent the sparkly silver dust spiralling off into the trees. "There," she said. "That'll do for a start. Let's see what's happening now."

The three friends flapped their wings and set off through the dark wood again. As they neared the clearing where their feast was taking place, a lovely smell drifted up to them. "Mmmm... They've got the sausages going!" Rachel realised, with a big grin.

"And look – you can see the campfire from here!" Kirsty exclaimed, pointing ahead, to where bright flames were blazing, making the twigs crackle and snap.

Morgan smiled. "I'll turn you back into girls, so you can join your friends and family," she said, waving her wand.

In the next moment, Kirsty and Rachel felt themselves growing all the way back to their usual sizes, with their feet firmly on the ground again. "Now, you were meant to be collecting more firewood, weren't you?" Morgan remembered.

"Here, this will save you a job."

She waved her wand again, and a pile of dry sticks and branches appeared in both Rachel's and Kirsty's arms.

"Perfect for the fire," Morgan smiled.

Then she kissed each girl on the cheek and waved goodbye. "I'd better fly around and check all the other midnight feasts are going as well as yours," she told them. "Thanks again – oh, and look out for a big surprise!"

And before the girls could ask what she meant, she had vanished.

Kirsty and Rachel dumped their firewood in a pile near Peter, and went back to their places at the campfire. "Marshmallow, girls?" Mrs Tate said, offering them the bag.

"Yes, please!" they chorused eagerly.

The rest of the midnight feast was great fun. Everyone enjoyed toasting (and eating!) the sweet gooey marshmallows, as well as tucking into sausages, potatoes and soup. Then there was just time for a campfire singsong before the midnight fireworks!

"Oooh!" "Ahhhh!" everyone sighed as bright flashes of colour glittered and glowed against the midnight sky. And then, just as Kirsty and Rachel thought the night couldn't get any more perfect, the last set of fireworks went off with an extraordinary

series of bangs…and some sparkly
writing appeared in the sky.

"Enjoy the Midnight Magic!" Peter
read aloud in surprise.

"Wow! How did that happen?"
someone asked.

Peter looked baffled. "I have no idea,"
he confessed, scratching his head.

Rachel and Kirsty grinned at
each other. They knew
that Morgan must
have 'helped' the
fireworks with
some of her
magic. But
that, of course,
was going to
stay their very
special secret!

### The Twilight Fairies

Now Rachel and Kirsty have helped
Morgan, it's time to help...

# Yasmin the Night Owl Fairy

# Night or Day?

"Hold on tight, Rachel," Kirsty called to her best friend, Rachel Walker. "We're almost there!"

"I'm right behind you, Kirsty!" Rachel called back.

The girls were walking carefully across the wobbly bridge that was strung between two trees in the Forest Fun adventure playground. The bridge was made of wooden slats with sturdy rope handles. It swayed and wobbled gently from side to side and up and down as the girls moved across it, making them shriek with laughter.

"Oh, this is just the best fun!" Kirsty panted. "I love Camp Stargaze, Rachel. There's so much to do here."

The girls and their parents were spending a week of the summer holidays at Camp Stargaze, and the Forest Fun playground was in a clearing in the woods just outside the camp. There was a treetop walk, several wildlife hides and two zip slides next to each other, as well as the wobbly bridge. The biggest tree in the clearing, the one the girls were heading to along the wobbly bridge, had a wooden treehouse in its branches. There was also a twisty slide wrapped around the tree's trunk that led down into an underground house under the roots of the tree. It was late afternoon, just after tea-time, and the girls were still enjoying the warmth of the summer sunshine.

"I know," Rachel agreed. "Camp Stargaze is brilliant. And not only that, we're in the middle of another exciting fairy adventure, too!"

When Rachel and Kirsty had arrived at the camp, their fairy friends had asked for their help once more. The girls had met the Twilight Fairies who were responsible for making sure that the hours between dusk and dawn were peaceful and harmonious in the human as well as the fairy worlds, with the help of their special bags of magical fairy dust. But while the Twilight Fairies were at a party under the stars, Jack Frost and his goblins had stolen the magic bags from the fairies! Jack Frost was determined to cause night-time chaos and so, with his icy magic, he'd sent the goblins to hide the bags away in the human world. But Rachel, Kirsty and the Twilight Fairies had already found four of the seven bags, and they were hoping to find the others, too.

"Rachel, Kirsty!" a voice shouted. "We're over here."

The girls glanced up and saw their new friends, Matt and Lucas, hanging out of one of the treehouse windows. Rachel and Kirsty wobbled their way to the end of the bridge and went to join them inside the treehouse.

"Have you been on the zip slides yet?" Lucas asked with a grin.

Kirsty shook her head. "I think I need to recover from the wobbly bridge, first!" she replied.

Matt was still hanging out of the window. "Look, Lucas," he said, pointing down at the ground below them. "There's your mum and Lizzy."

Lucas's mum and his little sister were wandering through the clearing. They waved up at the treehouse, and Lucas, Rachel, Kirsty and Matt waved back.

"Let's go down the twisty slide and say a proper hello!" Rachel suggested.

The top of the silver slide was just outside the treehouse door. Rachel climbed onto it and then immediately shot downwards with a shriek of surprise.

"It's really slippery!" she cried as she disappeared from view.

"Watch out, Rachel!" Kirsty yelled as she, too, jumped onto the slide. "Here I come!"

Laughing, Rachel whizzed around the trunk of the tree and then through the door of the underground house at the bottom of the tree. There she tumbled off the end of the slide onto a soft mat. Kirsty came flying into the underground house a few seconds later, and the two girls grinned at each other.

"Here come the boys!" Rachel remarked as they heard Matt and Lucas sliding towards them.

First Matt, and then Lucas, whizzed down into the underground house. Then all four of them climbed out and ran to join Lucas's mum and Lizzy. They were staring very intently at a large bush.

"What are you looking at?" Lucas asked curiously.

"Hedgehogs," Lucas's mum replied, her and Lizzy's eyes wide with delight. "Look!"

Rachel and Kirsty peered into the bottom of the bush, and saw two small hedgehogs scampering around among the leaves.

"Aren't they cute?" said Rachel as the hedgehogs scurried busily to and fro on their tiny paws.

Just then Kirsty heard a rustling noise in the undergrowth behind them. She spun round and caught a glimpse of grey fur and a black and white striped head. Quickly she nudged Rachel.

"There's a badger over there!" Kirsty whispered.

Rachel, Lucas and the others watched in amazement as the badger came into view. He was snuffling through the leaves in search of something to eat.

"This is great!" Matt said, looking very excited as the badger hurried past, taking no notice of them. "I've never seen a badger or a hedgehog in daylight before."

Kirsty frowned. "Matt's right," she said to Rachel. "Don't hedgehogs and badgers usually come out at night...?"

Read the rest of

# Yasmin
## the Night Owl Fairy

to find out what magic happens next...

Available now!

# Florence the Friendship Fairy

978-1-40831-238-4

£5.99

Can Kirsty and Rachel find the three lost magical items that Florence needs to keep friendship special?

Have you checked out the

# Meet the Showtime Fairies

## out now!

**Madison the Magic Show Fairy**
978-1-40831-286-5

**Leah the Theatre Fairy**
978-1-40831-287-2

**Alesha the Acrobat Fairy**
978-1-40831-288-9

**Darcey the Dance Diva Fairy**
978-1-40831-289-6

**Amelia the Singing Fairy**
978-1-40831-291-9

**Isla the Ice Star Fairy**
978-1-40831-292-6

**Taylor the Talent Show Fairy**
978-1-40831-290-2